Summary and Analysis of

1984

Based on the Book
by George Orwell

WORTH BOOKS
SMART SUMMARIES

This Worth Books book is based on the 2013 ebook edition of *1984* by George Orwell published by Martin Secker & Warburg Ltd.

Summary and analysis copyright © 2017 by Open Road Integrated Media, Inc.

ISBN: 978-1-5040-4680-0

Worth Books
180 Maiden Lane
Suite 8A
New York, NY 10038
www.worthbooks.com

WORTH BOOKS
SMART SUMMARIES

Worth Books is a division of Open Road Integrated Media, Inc.

Contents

Context

Written in the aftermath of World War II, and first published in 1949, George Orwell's *1984* is a dystopian novel warning of the dangers of life under a totalitarian government. The story is set in Airstrip One of Oceania—formerly London, England—after the Revolution.

Twelve years before the book's publication, Orwell worked as a BBC correspondent in Spain during Generalíssimo Francisco Franco's fascist regime. He and his wife took up arms alongside POUM (Partit Obrer d'Unificació Marxista), the Workers' Party of Marxist Unification. Orwell became disenchanted with journalism and the media, claiming they were a propaganda machine to disseminate lies to the masses, which would be a common theme running through his novels.

By the time of *1984*'s release, Adolf Hitler's Nazi Germany had been defeated, but the Communist Party was gaining traction in China, and iron curtains were cropping up around Josef Stalin's Soviet Union. Given the political climate and the increasing oppression of individual civil liberties, Orwell's story of Big Brother, protectionism, and institutional mind-control was particularly insightful and perhaps prescient.

According to the *New York Times*, there was a 9,500% increase in sales of the book over the course of five days in January 2017, most likely as the result of White House spokesperson Kellyanne Conway's use of the term "alternative facts" in an interview. The term struck many readers as being reminiscent of the "Newspeak" from *1984*.

Overview

Winston Smith is a sluggish, middle-aged man, a worn-out cog in the totalitarian machine called Oceania, which is one of three super-states remaining after the Revolution. Disillusioned about the ruling Inner Party, Winston is a low-ranking Outer Party member who works for the Ministry of Truth rewriting history. In April 1984, Winston begins a diary—an act, if discovered by the Thought Police, punishable by death. Wherever Winston goes, telescreens monitor his words, expressions, and movements. Gigantic posters of the post-Revolutionary leader are plastered all around the city with a caption that reads: "BIG BROTHER IS WATCHING YOU."

One day, during the Two Minutes Hate, an indoctrination session that stirs antipathy for a man named Emmanuel Goldstein who is considered an enemy of the State, Winston sees a pretty young comrade. He suspects she may be an agent for the Thought Police. Meanwhile, Winston hopes that a high-ranking Party official named O'Brien may be a member of an underground opposition movement called the Brotherhood.

A forbidden love affair soon develops between Winston and the young woman, whose name is Julia. For a while Winston's life seems tolerable. The couple secretly rents a room above a junk shop as their love nest. They decide to trust O'Brien and they finally get a chance to meet him.

Unfortunately, O'Brien turns out to be a Party government agent who set them up. Winston and Julia are arrested and incarcerated separately.

Physically tortured and reprogrammed through mind-control techniques, Winston betrays the woman he loves. After a protracted brainwashing, he becomes a listless, gin-dependent member of the Party, and an enthusiastic loyalist to Big Brother.

Cast of Characters

Ampleforth: Winston's coworker at the Records Department, Ampleforth's job is to remove objectionable text from poetry. He's imprisoned by the Party for leaving the word "God" in a Rudyard Kipling poem.

Big Brother: The omnipotent personification of the controlling Party of Oceania, the leader's likeness is found plastered on giant posters and broadcast on telescreens everywhere. An authoritative guise that might not physically exist, Big Brother's omnipresent avatar represents the constant intrusive surveillance of the masses.

Mr. Charrington: A kindly older gentleman and proprietor of the junk shop, Mr. Charrington represents a link to the fading memories of the past. He later rents the room upstairs to Winston and Julia. It turns out he's living a double life.

Emmanuel Goldstein: Enemy of the Party and exiled leader of the Brotherhood, Goldstein is a powerful and vilified symbol of the resistance.

Julia: Young and sensual, Julia is Winston's lover and confidant. She's practical, self-indulgent, and less interested in political revolt than pleasure—characteristics in contrast to Winston's commitment to the greater good.

O'Brien: Elusive and powerful, O'Brien is a high-ranking Inner Party member. Believed to be part of a clandestine anti-Party movement called the Brotherhood, he draws the rebellious Winston and Julia into the dark world of the insurgency before revealing his true allegiances.

Syme: Intelligent and dedicated, Syme works tirelessly developing language for the Party's Newspeak dictionary. His knowledge and expertise become a threat to the Party and he vanishes.

Tom Parsons: Genially oafish, Tom lives in a flat with his family in Winston's building, and is a colleague at the Ministry of Truth. Tom is a Party loyalist, though he fears his malicious, overindulged, indoctrinated children will one day betray him.

Winston Smith: The protagonist in the story, Winston is an intelligent common man. Though he works to create lies for the government, he despises their totalitarian control. Physically weak and past his prime, he's a dreamer with the heart of a revolutionary.

Summary

ONE

I

On a cold, windy April day in 1984, Winston Smith comes home at lunchtime from his job at the Ministry of Truth. He wears company-issued blue overalls and appears frail and older than his thirty-nine years. Because of a varicose ulcer in his ankle, the climb to his dingy, seventh-floor flat in the Victory Mansions is painful. Winston rests on the landings where enormous posters of a mustachioed man stare at him. The caption reads: BIG BROTHER IS WATCHING YOU.

Inside the apartment, Winston looks out the window at the towering white Ministry of Truth pyramid where he's employed as a clerk rewriting records. There are three other pyramids housing the Ministry of Peace (the war department), the Ministry of Love (the frightening department of law and order), and the Ministry of Plenty (the department of economic affairs). From a distance he sees the slogan inscribed on the Ministry of Truth's facade: WAR IS PEACE, FREEDOM IS SLAVERY, IGNORANCE IS STRENGTH.

Winston can't remember what London was like before it became the chief city of Airstrip One of Oceania. He pours a teacup of oily Victory Gin and sits in an alcove, his back to the ubiquitous telescreen, which can see and hear everything in range. He takes out a pen, a bottle of ink, and a blank book, and recalls the incident that triggered his decision to start a diary.

It was last week, at the Two Minutes Hate. He was surprised to see a dark-haired young woman and O'Brien, a high-ranking Inner Party member. Winston was wary of the too-attractive dark-haired woman, suspecting she might be an agent of the Thought Police. O'Brien, on the other hand, gave him the impression of being a counter-revolutionary. The Hate session began with a screeching noise, followed by the onscreen face of Emmanuel Goldstein, the Enemy of the People, along with Goldstein's bleating voice.

Goldstein is the commander of the Brotherhood, an underground network conspiring to overthrow the State. Winston felt loathing for the dark-haired girl, partially because she was pretty and sexless—a symbol of chastity common in young Party comrades. The Party expects him to hate Goldstein, but he views Goldstein as a guardian of truth and sanity in a world full of lies. Winston despises Big Brother, the Party, and the Thought Police, and prays the rumors of a growing resistance are true. At the Hate session, O'Brien's eyes met Winston's, and he thought it was a sign of their solidarity.

Back at his apartment, Winston scribbles down words in a stream of consciousness, then writes the phrase "DOWN WITH BIG BROTHER" over and over again. The act is punishable by death.

A knock at the door makes him jump.

Need to Know: Winston is on the threshold of joining the revolution, but he doesn't know how. If there are others who feel as rebellious as he does, the diary could be a way to preserve his memories for future readers—maybe O'Brien. The words in the diary are proof that something exists outside himself.

II

In his haste, Winston leaves the diary open on the table with the treasonous words in sight. He answers the door and finds Mrs. Parsons, his neighbor and the wife of his colleague Tom Parsons, in need of help unclogging her sink since her husband's at work. Inside the Parsons' flat, their two unruly children surround him with a menacing game of name-calling: "traitor," "thought-criminal," and "Goldstein." Their taunting unnerves him. Mrs. Parsons explains that the children are agitated because they can't go to the hanging at the park.

In the hall, returning back to his apartment, something stings the back of Winston's neck. He turns to see Mrs. Parsons pulling her son, holding a slingshot, back inside. The fear on her face is warranted, since every week a child reports his parent to the police.

Seven years earlier, Winston dreamed that a voice in the dark whispered, "We will meet in the place where there is no darkness." Now he recognizes the voice as O'Brien's, and wonders if it's a prophecy.

A bulletin over the telescreen reports that Party forces have won a glorious victory. Also chocolate rations will be reduced. Winston looks through the window down at the street where a poster with the word INGSOC (the sacred principles of the Party) flaps in the wind. Before Winston heads back to work, he writes, "Thoughtcrime does not entail death: thoughtcrime IS death." He washes the incriminating ink stains off his fingers and hides the diary in a drawer.

Need to Know: Thought used to be free and truth used to exist. Now conformity and uniformity are required. Big Brother controls everything—even thoughts. Without personal freedoms people are essentially dead.

III

When Winston was eleven years old, his mother, father, and baby sister disappeared—probably swallowed up by the purge of the 1950s. He often imagines his family sucked down into a deep well or watery grave. One night, he dreams of a green pasture and the dark-haired girl walking toward him, tearing off her clothes. He wakes with the word "Shakespeare" on his lips, just as the telescreen whistles and announces that Physical Jerks (daily exercises) begin in three minutes. Winston crawls out of bed and labors to follow the rhythmic movements of the woman on the telescreen.

Winston remembers only bits and pieces of his childhood, before the country was at war and when Airstrip One was called England, Britain, or London. Today Oceania is at war with Eastasia and Eurasia. Reality is controlled by the principles of "Newspeak" and "doublethink." Knowledge only exists in consciousness, so when the Party erases history and replaces it with a fable, it's acceptable to the masses.

Need to Know: Working for the Ministry of Truth means Winston must live in a state of knowing and not knowing: conscious of the truth, while telling the Party's carefully constructed lies.

IV

Inside Winston's cubicle at the Records Department are three orifices: a small tube for written messages, a larger one for newspapers, and a wide slit covered by wire grating for scrap paper. Nicknamed "memory holes," documents slated for destruction are dropped in the slots and incinerated in furnaces. Winston's job entails rewriting Party statements and promises. He substitutes the facts with new and corrected ones. Newspapers, books, magazines, leaflets, films, photographs—any type of documentation— are corrected to fit the new reality according to the Party. Burning the original text makes it impossible to prove falsification has taken place. A lie becomes the truth.

His cubicle is located in a windowless hall among rows of identical cubicles filled with swarms of workers engaging in a multitude of jobs. Most of them he doesn't know by name. Today Winston receives an assignment to rewrite a speech by Big Brother. He invents a war hero to commemorate named Captain Ogilvy, adds a few lines to the speech, and inserts a fake photograph. With a single act of forgery, a new man is brought into existence.

Need to Know: The Party washes and rewrites history, substituting facts with their own propaganda. Statistics are fantasies and people who've been vaporized are deleted as if they never lived. Every piece of information fades away into a shadowy world of uncertainty.

V

At the canteen, Winston sits with Syme, an intelligent man working on the Eleventh Edition of the Newspeak Dictionary. His job is to destroy words, not invent them. He says someday Oldspeak (current English) will be obsolete and Newspeak will replace it. Controlling language narrows one's range of thought. Obliterating literature from the past creates a new climate of belief. Soon there will be no need to think at all.

Tom Parsons joins them and apologizes to Winston for the slingshot incident. He launches into a boastful story about how his young daughter turned a stranger in for wearing funny shoes. The Thought Police can pick up on the slightest thing: A change in facial expression, a nervous tic, or letting your mind wander. Anything can give you away. Winston fakes a smile, but he's disturbed by Tom's story.

A new bulletin over the telescreen announces that Oceania's standard of living has gone up twenty percent, and chocolate rations are increasing. Winston wonders if he's the only one who remembers that yesterday they said chocolate rations were decreasing.

The dark-haired girl at the next table turns and looks at Winston, arousing suspicion that she's spying on him.

Need to Know: Language is systematically being eliminated by the government, while Winston and his coworkers continue to invent scenarios of progress and victory that don't exist.

VI

In his diary, Winston reconstructs an encounter with a prostitute three years earlier that still torments him. The Party forbids consorting with prostitutes, but doesn't dole out too serious a punishment. It's promiscuity between Party members that is considered a serious crime. The unspoken aim of the Party is not to prevent men and women from forming loyalties, but to remove the aspect of pleasure from the sexual act. Marriage must be preapproved, and couples attracted to one another are usually denied. Intercourse is for the sole purpose of producing children.

Winston and his wife, Katharine, were married for

fifteen months. She was the most stupid, vulgar, and empty-minded person he'd ever met, but he'd have stayed with her if it hadn't been for the sex. She was a wooden board who submitted to him with her eyes shut. When no child was conceived, they agreed to part ways. What Winston wants more than anything is to be loved, and to break down a woman's wall of Party-ingrained virtue.

Need to Know: The Party's goal is to kill an individual's sexual instinct, and barring that, to distort erotic impulses. From an early age, women are indoctrinated in the belief that chastity is a noble attribute that proves their loyalty to the government. Big Brother considers lust a thoughtcrime.

VII

Winston is convinced that hope for the future lies in the proles, the working class of Oceania. Overthrowing the government from inside the Party would be impossible, so it would have to come from outside. Proles are in the perfect position for revolt because they haven't been indoctrinated into the Party's ideology, and the civil police hardly ever interfere with them, even though they make up 85% of the population. If proles organized and channeled their energy toward political rebellion, they'd have a chance.

Winston pulls out a children's history book borrowed from Mrs. Parsons and begins copying down a detailed description of London before the Revolution, when capitalists ruled. Capitalists owned all the land, money, houses, and factories. Everyone was a slave. Winston has no tangible evidence that these facts are untrue, but he feels it in his gut. The Party line about the city's current success is directly contradicted by what Winston witnesses on the streets, with people shuffling around in leaky shoes and sleeping in rundown housing. The telescreens constantly spew statistics about prosperity, while erasing the proof about what's really going on. For thirty seconds in 1973, Winston held proof of the Party's corruption in his hand. He found a photograph of concrete evidence that three men convicted of treason were innocent. If the photo were ever to get out, it would have destroyed the Party. Not wanting to be arrested, Winston threw the photo into the memory hole, but he'll never forget the image nor the date the snapshot was taken.

Winston knows how the Party falsifies the past, but he doesn't understand why. He believes that O'Brien is in agreement with him. How could anyone not know that the natural world exists and the laws of nature don't change? Stones are hard, water is wet, and freedom means you can say aloud "two plus two makes four."

Need to Know: Proles are a large, untapped socio-economic group with the potential power to abolish the Party, partly because they're beneath suspicion, and partly because they're free to live their lives. But the proles show little sign of wanting change.

VIII

While on a detour through a prole neighborhood, formerly the northeast slums of London, Winston admires the simpler lives in the rundown area, especially when he smells real coffee brewing.

Someone shouts, "Steamer!" which is a nickname for a rocket bomb. Everyone scatters, and Winston ducks for cover. He survives the blast, dusts himself off, and continues walking. He finds a bloodied hand severed at the wrist and nonchalantly kicks the stump into the gutter.

A few blocks away from the bombsite, pubs are teeming with customers as if nothing had happened. He buys an old man a drink and asks him about what life was like before the Revolution. The old man's recollection is a rubbish heap of details, so Winston gives up and returns to the street.

Wandering aimlessly, he finds himself in front of a junk shop where he'd bought the diary years before. After quickly ducking inside, Winston is greeted by the shop owner, Mr. Charrington. Most of the wares on display are trash, but Winston finds an appealing antique paperweight made of glass and coral. It's a beautiful object from the past.

Mr. Charrington shows Winston a room upstairs that has an armchair, a bed, and a fireplace. On the wall is a picture of a building in a frame that Winston finds familiar. Mr. Charrington explains that it was a church, and recites a rhyme about it, "Oranges and lemons, say the bells of St. Clement's." Winston likes the room's feeling of nostalgia—a sort of ancestral memory. He promises himself he'll return.

Back on the street, Winston is shocked to see the dark-haired woman walking toward him. She passes without saying a word, but now he's sure she's following him.

At home, Winston takes out his diary, but can't concentrate. All he can think about is the torture he might be subjected to if he's caught. He tries to conjure up the face of O'Brien, but Big Brother pops into his head instead.

Need to Know: There are few people remaining from the old days and many are too senile to remember the past. Worse, what they recall is scattered and useless. Once memories fail and written records are extinguished, there will be no standard against which to prove the truth.

TWO

I

Four days have passed since Winston saw the dark-haired woman near the junk shop. Now, in a corridor of the Ministry of Truth, she's heading toward him with her arm in a sling. As she reaches him, she trips and falls, letting out a cry of pain. Winston helps her up and asks if she's hurt. She says she's fine, thanks him, and continues on her way. In the few seconds it took to help her up, the girl slipped a scrap of paper into his hand. It reads, "I love you."

Winston can't focus on work, and figures out a plan to talk to the young woman. It's possible she's setting a trap, but he's willing to take that risk. He'll approach her at the canteen at lunchtime. Several days pass before he finally manages to find an empty seat next to her. They arrange a clandestine meeting that night at Victory Square.

Standing shoulder to shoulder in a dense crowd of people, the woman whispers instructions for a rendezvous Sunday afternoon. She squeezes Winston's hand.

Need to Know: Winston is willing to put his life in jeopardy for a chance to have a love affair with the dark-haired woman.

II

There are no telescreens in the countryside, but it's still dangerous. Winston meets the dark-haired woman and they silently walk down a wooded path to a grassy knoll in a clearing. Soon she's in his arms, kissing him and using terms of endearment, but they stop short of lovemaking. Her name is Julia and she's been with hundreds of men. Because Winston hates pure and virtuous women, that revelation makes him more drawn to her.

Need to Know: Pure love or lust no longer exists in the Party. Emotions are always mixed with fear and hatred. Sex is a political act of defiance.

III

Julia is twenty-six years old, lives in a hostel with thirty other young women, and works on novel-writing machines in the Fiction Department. The only person she knew who was alive before the Revolution was her grandfather. He died when she was eight. She's a good comrade, and once worked producing porn for distribution among the proles. Only women worked in Pornosec, because the Party considered men's sexual instincts less controllable. Julia breaks Party rules for her own pleasure—she's not interested in political revolt. She believes it's possible to live the way you want and she won't tolerate negative talk of dying.

Need to Know: The sexual impulse is dangerous to the Party, just like parental instincts, which explains why children are systematically removed from their parents once they're old enough. The family is an extension of the Thought Police.

IV

Winston knows how dangerous it is to rent the room above the junk shop, but with the difficulty of arranging regular liaisons with Julia, he has no other choice.

Julia enters the room carrying a canvas bag containing Inner Party contraband, including sugar, coffee, white bread, a pot of jam, and tea. She tells Winston to turn around because she has a surprise for him. When he looks back, she's put on makeup and looks pretty and feminine. They strip naked and make love. Afterward, they sleep wrapped in each other's arms and Winston wonders if there was a time when such a thing was ordinary.

Suddenly, Julia throws a shoe into the corner. A rat has poked his nose out of a hole in the wainscoting and Winston turns white, horrified. He relives a recurring nightmare he's had throughout his life. In the dream, he stands in front of a wall of darkness, knowing what's behind it, but deceiving himself that the thing is unendurable, too dreadful to be faced. He hates rats.

Need to Know: Privacy is extremely valuable. Their rented room is like the glass paperweight Winston bought in an earlier chapter, and Julia is the coral inside the glass—liberated and fixed in an eternity of their own making.

V

Syme has been absent from work, so Winston checks if his name is on the list of Chess Committee members. It's not. Syme has simply vanished and ceased to exist.

Preparations for Hate Week are underway. Staff from all of the Ministries work overtime, rocket bombs explode at regular intervals, and the newest Hate Week theme song plays incessantly on the telescreen. For Winston and Julia, the room over the junk shop is paradise. Winston's health improves as life becomes more tolerable. They are in love and fantasize about a future together, although they know there's no escape. Winston tells Julia that he thinks O'Brien is an enemy of the Party. She doesn't find it too farfetched.

Need to Know: History is fading away, and almost nothing is known about the years before the Revolution. All records are being destroyed, books are being rewritten, pictures are repainted, and dates altered. Every minute more history disappears.

VI

For seven years, Winston has wanted to meet O'Brien face to face, and now they are actually speaking to one another. O'Brien gives Winston his address under the pretense that he will come by to pick up the newest edition of the Party's dictionary. The conspiracy that Winston has dreamed about exists.

Need to Know: Winston feels apprehensive about making a move against Big Brother. He knows the consequences will be fatal, yet he's compelled to go forward.

VII

Winston wakes in tears from a bad dream. He used to think that he'd murdered his own mother, but the dream brought back memories about what actually happened.

After his father disappeared, his mother became spiritless. She fulfilled her motherly duties, but was otherwise a zombie. There wasn't much food to eat, so Winston badgered her for more than his share, even if it meant his baby sister went without. One day, they received a three-ounce rationing of chocolate, which his mother divided into thirds. Winston whined and nagged until she gave him two-thirds of the bar. The other third went to his sister. Winston snatched the chocolate from the baby's hand and ran from the house. When he returned later that evening, his mother and sister had disappeared.

Winston misses the time when his feelings were his own, and were not influenced by the Party. Proles were able to hold onto their humanity. Party members could be tortured into telling everything that they thought and did. The only impregnable thing left in the world was one's inner heart.

Need to Know: The Party robs people of power over the material world, but despite all their cleverness, they are still unable to read minds.

VIII

Winston and Julia are thrilled to be standing in the same room as the elusive O'Brien. The Inner Party member didn't look up from his desk when his servant escorted them inside. Winston worries going there may have been a serious error in judgment.

O'Brien turns off his telescreen, which Winston didn't know was possible. Apparently, that's a privilege of O'Brien's rank.

He and Julia declare their allegiance to the enemies of the State and admit to being thought-criminals and adulterers. O'Brien and his butler invite the couple to sit down and share a glass of wine with them. O'Brien proposes a toast to their leader, Emmanuel Goldstein.

After confirming that the Brotherhood indeed exists, O'Brien fires off a battery of questions about their willingness to do anything for the cause. The one thing they won't do is separate from one another. O'Brien commends them on their honesty and explains the conditions of membership to the Brotherhood. *The book*, written by Goldstein, is required reading and will be dispatched by secret courier. Once they've finished reading it, they'll be full-fledged members of the Brotherhood. Before saying goodbye, they raise their glasses again and Winston toasts, "To the past."

Julia leaves first. Before walking out the door, Winston asks O'Brien if he knows an old rhyme that starts with "Oranges and lemons," and O'Brien chants, "say the bells of St. Clement's."

Need to Know: The Brotherhood cannot be wiped out because it's not organized in the traditional way. They won't see any real changes in their lifetime. All they can hope for is to extend the area of sanity a little.

IX

Winston is exhausted from working ninety hours in the last five days. He walks down the street toward Mr. Charrington's shop, carrying the briefcase with *the book* inside. It's the sixth day of Hate Week, and after years of stirring up a frenzy of disgust for the enemy of Eurasia, the Party announces that Oceania is at war with Eastasia, but Eurasia is its ally. The hate continues, but the target has changed.

What this meant for Winston was that all political literature of the last five years was now obsolete and had to be rewritten. Records Department employees were called to their posts and worked eighteen hours a day, with only snatches of sleep permitted. It was crushing work that would ultimately make it impossible for anyone to prove that a war with Eurasia had ever happened.

Winston sits in the armchair and opens his briefcase. The heavy, black volume inside has no writing on the cover, but the title page reads, "THE THEORY AND PRACTICE OF OLIGARCHICAL COLLECTIVISM by Emmanuel Goldstein."

Winston begins reading *the book* chapter by chapter, stopping occasionally to reflect on how amazing it is that he's reading alone without a telescreen.

He learns that the world is broken up into three super-states, and that wars today involve very few soldiers and produce less casualties than in the past. This is because the three super-states are self-contained economies and have little need to compete with each other for raw materials.

In the nineteenth century (the age of the machine), automation had the potential to raise the standard of living. The Party realized that an even distribution of wealth threatened its hierarchical society, so the government needed to find a way to keep industry turning without increasing wealth. Goods had to be produced, but not distributed. Their solution was to create continuous wars to use up surplus materials. As a result, the world is more primitive than it was fifty years ago.

The Party's two main concerns are: 1.) Knowing what another person is thinking, and 2.) Being able to kill millions of people in a few seconds. The three super-states possess atomic bombs, but they have an informal agreement not to drop them on one another. The main objective is for war to continue eternally.

The book is fascinating and confirms everything Winston believed. When Julia arrives, he reads to her out loud. Julia falls asleep. He closes the book and pulls the covers over them.

Need to Know: If leisure and security were enjoyed by all, then the poor and illiterate would learn to think for themselves. This is death to a hierarchical society, which can only survive when there's a privileged minority with a base of poverty and ignorance beneath them.

X

Winston abruptly wakes when a voice comes from behind the picture frame on the wall, which falls to the floor revealing a hidden telescreen. A stampede of boots clomps up the stairs, and large men in black uniforms break into the room. The men smash the glass paperweight. One violently kicks Winston in the ankle. Another man punches Julia in the solar plexus, and she collapses. The men carry her off.

Shocking Winston even more, Mr. Charrington strides in, barking orders at the black-clad men. Winston realizes that he's looking at an agent of the Thought Police.

Need to Know: Mr. Charrington is physically transformed from the old man that Winston knew. He's much taller and bigger, and his white hair has turned black. The wrinkles are gone, revealing a ominous man of thirty-five. As Winston feared, the Thought Police are insidious, clever, and everywhere.

THREE

I

Winston assumes he's in a windowless cell at the Ministry of Love. The cell has a shelf, a lavatory pan, and four telescreens—one on each wall. He hasn't been fed since his arrest.

Earlier he'd been in a filthy holding facility shared by political prisoners and common criminals. Two women Party members whispered worriedly to one other about something called "Room 101."

The men in boots bring his colleague, the poet Ampleforth, into the cell. The man is in shambles and doesn't recognize Winston at first. Ampleforth isn't sure why he was arrested, but he believes it was because he left the word "God" in a Rudyard Kipling poem.

An officer waves to Ampleforth and says, "Room 101," and the guards escort him out. Later the cell opens again and Parsons is ushered inside. He's been detained for committing a thoughtcrime. In his sleep he uttered the words, "Down with Big Brother," so his daughter reported him. Parsons is taken away, too.

A steady stream of prisoners flows in and out. One woman turns completely white when she's assigned to Room 101, then another man, apparently starving to death, turns a sickly green when Room 101 is mentioned. Begging not to be taken back there, he offers his wife and children up for slaughter, but the guards drag him out of the cell anyway.

Finally, O'Brien enters and Winston gasps, "They've got you too!" But O'Brien replies that they got him a long time ago, and Winston realizes that he's always known that to be true. A blow to Winston's elbow knocks him to his knees, and he thinks there's nothing worse in the world than physical pain.

Need to Know: Winston dimly thinks of Julia, wondering what sort of treatment she's enduring. He asks himself if he could save Julia by doubling his pain, would he? Intellectually he answers, "Yes," but in the face of real pain, he decides there are no heroes.

II

Winston is strapped to a cot, while O'Brien and a man with a white lab coat and a hypodermic syringe stand over him. Winston remembers regular interrogation and torture that became less frequent and was replaced by threats of violence and merciless questioning by bespectacled Party intellectuals in twelve-hour stretches. Winston's sole goal is to find out what they want to know and confess to it. Whether it's murder, embezzlement, or sexual perversion, it doesn't matter. He'll admit to anything.

O'Brien, in control of the pain levers, applies a frightening agony that shoots through Winston's body. He's told that the jolt was at 40%, and the levers go all the way up to 100%. Winston knows he's being reprogrammed to doublethink, but he's overwhelmed by the pain.

As a test, O'Brien holds up four fingers and asks Winston to agree that there are five. He turns up the pain meter until Winston admits to seeing five fingers. Winston is rewarded with an injection that soothes the pain until it's almost forgotten. He feels love and gratitude for O'Brien.

O'Brien says that Winston isn't there merely for confessions or punishment. He's there to be transformed. The Party isn't interested in making martyrs out of their enemies. They'd rather convert them than kill them. They intend to squeeze Winston until he's empty of feelings. They affix a machine to his head that painlessly removes part of his brain, and Winston loses years of memories.

Winston is given the opportunity to ask questions, so he wants to know if Julia was tortured, if Big Brother exists, if Big Brother will ever die, and whether the Brotherhood is real. The last question is left unanswered—an unsolved riddle in his mind. He has one more question, which is, "What's in Room 101?" O'Brien says Winston already knows the answer. An injection into his arm sinks him into sleep.

Need to Know: The nagging voices break Winston down more completely than the black-uniformed men with boots and fists ever could. When the Party finishes brainwashing their enemies, there's nothing left except apologies and a love for Big Brother. They're made "clean" before they're vaporized.

III

The three stages of Winston's reintegration include learning, understanding, and acceptance. The second stage uses the pain lever infrequently, if at all. O'Brien teaches Winston that the Party doesn't seek power for the good of majority, but for its own sake. If people can escape their identities and merge with the Party, then they are the Party, powerful and immortal. Only individuals can be defeated.

Winston refuses to agree that any organization can control climate, gravity, disease, pain, and death. O'Brien insists that the Party controls the laws of nature, and he dismisses the existence of the universe and all of science. There's nothing that exists outside of man's consciousness, for it's not power over things the Party wields but power over men. Soon family relationships and sexual pleasure will be eradicated. There will be no laughter, art, literature, or science. Goldstein will exist forever, only so that he can be repeatedly defeated. Even under threat of severe pain, Winston won't believe O'Brien's assertions.

Frustrated with Winston's stubbornness, O'Brien orders him to strip naked and stand before a mirror. Winston is shocked and horrified by his own reflection. He's become a grey, crooked thing. His body is emaciated beyond recognition. His only consolation is that after all he's been through, he's never betrayed Julia. He's never stopped loving her.

Need to Know: The masses are made up of frail creatures who can't handle liberty or truth, so they must be ruled by those stronger than they are. Until a conversion is successful, one will endure torturous treatment for an interminable amount of time.

IV

Winston grows physically stronger every day. He's been given the comforts of a pillow, a mattress, and a stool in his cell. He's allowed to wash himself in a basin with warm water, and his varicose ulcer has been treated. He lost track of time, but he's fed on a regular basis, and he's able to exercise. His dreams are happy and he feels satisfied.

Winston has capitulated to the Party's beliefs as much as he is able. The fight is almost out of him. He's onboard with his reeducation, which he finds relatively easy now that he stopped swimming against the current. Winston is practicing Crimestop, which is an automatic, instinctive retreat into a mental blind spot to hide from dangerous thoughts, and he trains himself not to contradict the principles of the Party. However, when he cries out Julia's name, the men in boots punish his outburst. Winston has surrendered his mind, but he still hasn't given up his heart. O'Brien can tell that Winston doesn't love Big Brother, so the reintegration must start over again. "Room 101," O'Brien orders.

Need to Know: Winston has reached the point where he believes his contrary memories are false memories, yet he finds stupidity difficult to obtain. If he's to succeed, he must keep his hatred for Big Brother locked up deep inside, unconnected from the rest of himself. To die hating Big Brother is freedom.

V

In Room 101, a table is set a meter in front of Winston and another table is near the door. He's strapped into a chair, unable to move. O'Brien enters and explains that Room 101 contains "the worst thing in the world," although that thing is specific to each individual.

A cage is placed on the table with two rats inside. O'Brien says that when the rats are released, they will quickly devour Winston's flesh. Eyes first, he guesses. Winston screams like an animal, momentarily going insane. The rats are moved so near his face that he can smell their putrid odor. His worst nightmare has come true, and his only hope is to place another body between himself and the rats. He shouts frantically, "Do it to Julia! Not me!" The cage door clicks shut.

Need to Know: Every human being has a breaking point, but it doesn't always involve physical pain. Some things are unendurable and cannot be withstood. In the face of those things, a person will do almost anything required to achieve relief.

VI

Winston sits in his usual corner gazing up at the familiar face on the opposite wall. The caption reads, "BIG BROTHER IS WATCHING YOU." The waiter fills his glass with Victory Gin while the telescreen plays music. Winston waits for news from the African front. He swallows the gin with a shudder. Its oily scent reminds him of things that were once near his face. He can't name them, but the smell clings to his nostrils.

Since his release, he's gained some weight and has more color. The waiter brings over a chessboard, and a current issue of the *Times* with the page turned open to a chess problem. Seeing Winston's glass is empty, he fills it up again. Winston studies the chess problem, although he knows that white always checkmates. Always.

A voice on the telescreen says that news of the highest order will be announced shortly. Winston hopes to hear a good report about the war in Africa. His thoughts wander as he unconsciously draws $2 + 2 = 5$ with his fingertip on the dusty tabletop.

Winston has seen and spoken to Julia once. He spotted her at the park and followed her until they were standing side-by-side. He didn't kiss her, but he put his hand around her waist. It felt like stone. They both admitted that they'd betrayed one another, and that all they cared about had been saving themselves. Afterwards, it was impossible to feel the love they once had shared.

Winston wants to walk Julia as far as the Tube station, but he loses sight of her in the crowd. He returns to the cafe where it's warm. The waiter dutifully fills his empty glass with gin. Gin is his life. It sinks him into a stupor at night and wakes him up every morning. Twice a week he goes to the Ministry of Truth to work at his high-paying job, but work doesn't matter to him anymore.

He remembers a time when he was about ten or eleven years old. It was before his mother disappeared and they were a happy family. He pushes the image out of his mind, knowing it's a false memory. He jumps up at the sound of the trumpet coming from the telescreen. Oceania has won a great victory!

He thinks back on his time at the Ministry of Love when everything was forgiven and his soul was made white as snow. He gazes up affectionately at the poster of the enormous face in front of him. It's taken him forty years, but everything is all right now. The struggle is over. Winston has been victorious over himself. He loves Big Brother.

Need to Know: It was once believed that the Party couldn't get inside a person's mind, but what happens inside the Ministry of Love lasts forever. There are some things from which a person can never recover.

Character Analysis

Julia: Julia, Winston's love interest and confidante, is a survivor who has developed a keen sense of self-preservation. She rarely concerns herself about the plight of her comrades. She's skeptical, cunning, and resourceful, using the Party unapologetically to her advantage and pleasure. Julia's blatant sexuality is in direct conflict with the Party's goal to extinguish erotic instincts in its members. Most importantly, Julia's character provides Winston the motivation he needs to live and fight.

O'Brien: Representing the shadowy, duplicitous nature of the dystopian society of Oceania, O'Brien is the charismatic and mysterious main antagonist of the story. Aloof and calculating, O'Brien tortures his subjects with cold, vicious precision—a mirror of the regime he serves. As an unwavering loyalist of the Party, there's nothing he won't do to maintain his position of power, though at times he seems to feel a certain respect and admiration for Winston's intelligence and tough-mindedness in resisting his brainwashing. O'Brien is the personification of blind ambition and man's thirst for domination.

Winston Smith: The protagonist and moral center of the novel, Winston Smith is a low-level member of the Outer Party coping with the hypocrisy of hating the government's lies while working diligently to oil their propaganda machine. He's the embodiment of the common man fighting to maintain his dignity and humanity under totalitarian rule. His downfall stems from his naiveté in believing democracy, privacy, and individualism are rights owed to everyone, and that he has a chance to win them back once they've been taken away. Underneath Winston's weak, physical exterior—exemplifying the suffering he endures as a normal citizen—lies an intelligent man who dreams of joining the rebellion. Even when he falls in love and life seems almost tolerable, he still strives for greater freedom and affiliates himself with the Brotherhood whose aim is to overthrow Big Brother.

Winston underestimates the infinite power, reach, and boundless loyalty for the Party, so it's a struggle he ultimately loses. Reprogrammed and reindoctrinated with the ideologies of the iron-fisted government, he lives out the rest of his life as a true-blue servant of the tyrannical state he once despised. In the end, Winston becomes a symbol of hopelessness against an unstoppable force.

Themes and Symbols

Themes

Mind control/Brainwashing: A scientific practice of conversion therapy, in which human beings are subjected to a battery of stimuli, such as torture, fear, threats, and subliminal suggestions, in order to force them to succumb to certain thoughts or beliefs. In the book, there are several kinds of mind-control techniques at play. The most widespread uses telescreens to remind citizens that there's always someone watching or listening to everything they do and say. With this constant level of fear instilled in the lower classes, they stay in line. Once Winston is arrested for thoughtcrime, he's subjected to a protracted torture regimen, which eventually breaks him down. With all the emotion squeezed out of him, he becomes a blank slate on which the Party can redraw him into a loyal, zombielike follower.

Propaganda: The politically motivated use of biased or false information intended to influence the hearts and minds of a population. The Records Department at the Ministry of Truth produces blatantly false facts, erases history, and manipulates language to benefit those in the ruling class, while keeping lower classes powerless. The Party systematically creates an alternate reality so that normal citizens are unaware of their true circumstances and would have no reason to wage a revolution. Orwell's 1984 became a classic and cautionary tale of the dangers of allowing rightwing governments to wield unfettered power and influence, and a cultural touchstone about the pernicious omnipresence of propaganda.

Totalitarianism: A cult-like political state that uses oppressive means to control the masses. In the story, Big Brother is the supreme dictator of the Party, wielding power through an elaborate system of surveillance, thought-control, speech restrictions, protectionism, and class injustice. At the time of the writing of the book, Nazi Germany had ended, but communism and Stalinism were on the rise. The striking image of Big Brother looming over the city of Oceania underscores the danger of dictatorships taking control of every aspect of life, including political, economic, social, and cultural. Orwell feared that the world was at risk of losing free access to science, education, and art under these types of governments.

Symbols

Big Brother: The (possibly nonexistent) leader of the regime, Big Brother symbolizes the malevolent father figure who ceaselessly subjects his minions to surveillance as a direct warning not to contradict him or his ideology. Any infraction has severe consequences. His image on posters serves as an emblem of an abusive governmental power that dismantles civil liberties and eliminates personal privacy while providing the focal point of a leader to admire.

The glass paperweight: The beautiful glass and coral paperweight represents Winston and Julia's own private oasis, a secret, internal world where they're free to dream of the future. The antique trinket also represents a link to the forgotten past. With few people left who remember what life was like before the Revolution, history will soon be lost forever. The smashing of the paperweight is akin to the destruction of historical knowledge—without the context of history to inform them, the citizens of Oceania are subject only to the false "truth" put forth by the Party.

Rats: Rats are an archetypal symbol of evil, filth, and pestilence, but for Winston, the rat also presents a nightmarish wall of darkness, behind which lurks something unendurable and unnamed. It was his mortal fear of rats that proved to be Winston's ultimate downfall. Since rats are stereotypically associated with a vicious selfishness (rats devouring babies is mentioned in *1984*) and a sort of opportunistic survival instinct (rats abandoning a sinking ship, for instance) we can infer that Winston's memory of stealing the last bit of food from his baby sister instills a sense of guilt in him—in his desperation and hunger, he was no better than a rat.

Direct Quotes and Analysis

"You had to live—did live, from habit that became instinct—in the assumption that every sound you made was overheard, and, except in darkness, every movement scrutinized."

There was no way of knowing when and where the Thought Police were listening in, so Winston had to assume that everything he did, said, and even dreamed was being monitored. Home was not a refuge and everywhere Winston looked he saw a gigantic poster of Big Brother to remind him of the constant surveillance. The constant lack of unmonitored freedom squelches Winston's interior self to the point where he feels he must rebel or die.

"Asleep or awake, working or eating, indoors or out of doors, in the bath or in bed—no escape. Nothing was your own except the few cubic centimetres inside your skull."

Winston knew how strong and seemingly invulnerable the government was. He wondered why and for whom he was writing the diary: the future or the past? He knew it was inevitable that the diary would someday be burned to ashes and he would be vaporized. There's irony in the idea that Winston believed that a part of his mind was inviolable by the Party, when in fact they do manage to control his consciousness in the end.

"Day by day and almost minute by minute the past was brought up to date."

Winston's job at the Ministry of Truth was to ensure that every historical revision made by the Party would be reflected in newspapers, journals, books, and film. History was deleted and rewritten as the Party deemed fit. Once the falsification was finalized, the original document would be burned, making it impossible to prove any change had ever taken place. Without proof that the government was lying, their lies became the truth. Because he was constantly rewriting reality, Winston knew that nothing he did had any connection with the actual world. Statistics were made up by people like himself. Facts were just carefully constructed lies.

"Until they become conscious they will never rebel, and until after they have rebelled they cannot become conscious."

The vicious cycle of the proles: a group of working-class people who possessed the power to overthrow Big Brother and the Party, but who first must recognize the need for a revolution. Winston, in many ways, envies the proles, for he sees that they have managed to hold on to their humanity. He believes they are the country's only hope, but relying on them to change the world is a long shot.

"When you make love you're using up energy; and afterwards you feel happy and don't give a damn about anything. They can't bear you to feel like that."

Julia explains to Winston that the Party is against members having sexual relationships because they'd prefer people to save their energies for marching, cheering, and waving flags. If Party members are happy and content within themselves, they won't be enthusiastic and single-minded about serving their leader.

"To talk to him was like listening to the tinkling of a worn-out music-box. He had dragged out from the corners of his memory some more fragments of forgotten rhymes."

Winston found that talking with Mr. Charrington about the scraps of rubbish in his shop was like being with an extinct animal. He experienced a feeling of nostalgia from being around the old man, thinking that Charrington was a direct line to the disappearing past, the last of his kind. Winston knows that, sadly, soon Mr. Charrington's memories of history would be lost forever.

"It is deliberate policy to keep even the favoured groups somewhere near the brink of hardship, because a general state of scarcity increases the importance of small privileges and this magnified the distinction between one group and another."

Even privileged members of the Inner Party live in austerity and labor—one station up from the Outer Party members, who themselves still have a status above the proles. People in Oceania live in an atmosphere where the slightest enjoyment draws a distinction between wealth and poverty. In this social atmosphere, along with the consciousness of being engaged in constant war, people willingly hand over power to a small group of leaders.

Trivia

1. Among the words and phrases coined or popularized by George Orwell's *1984* are "doublespeak," "thoughtcrime," and, most famously, "Big Brother."

2. Ironically, according to the American Library Association, Orwell's *1984* is among the top ten most banned books in the world.

3. The term "English Socialism" (Ingsoc) that appears in the novel was originally used in Orwell's 1941 essay, "The Lion and the Unicorn: Socialism and the English Genius."

4. There have been many songs inspired by *1984*, including "2 + 2 = 5" by Radiohead, "Testify" by Rage Against the Machine, and "1984" by David Bowie.

5. Apple's "1984" iconic Super Bowl commercial is based on Orwell's science fiction novel. The spot is credited with changing product advertising forever.

6. George Orwell modeled "Room 101" after a BBC conference room where he spent many tedious hours while working for the Ministry of Information.

7. The formula used to test whether Winston has surrendered to the Party, "2 + 2 = 5," was an actual slogan used by the Communist Party of the Soviet Union.

8. Three years before writing *1984*, George Orwell penned a letter to Noel Willmett, explaining the premise of his novel.

9. Dictionary.com defines Orwellian "as an adjective, of, pertaining to, characteristic of, or resembling the literary work of George Orwell or the totalitarian future described in his antiutopian novel *1984* (1949)."

10. Between 1941 and 1943, Orwell, already a well-known anarchist, worked as a propagandist for the BBC, and later became literary editor of the left-leaning *Tribune* magazine.

What's That Word?

Crimestop: An automatic, instinctive mental blindspot to protect Party members from dangerous thoughts.

Doublethink: A term in Newspeak that describes Party members who are willing to believe carefully constructed lies by the government, and take part in the deliberate destruction of facts in order to rewrite history.

Ingsoc: Short for English Socialism, which refers to the sacred principles of the Party.

Newspeak: Deemed the official language of the Party, it's designed to narrow thought and render current English (Oldspeak) obsolete.

Speakwrite: A machine that transcribes speech into written text.

Telescreens: Television monitors/listening devices used by the Thought Police to conduct twenty-four hour surveillance on Oceania's citizens.

Thoughtcrime: Any thought, emotion, or expression that is contrary to the tenets and teachings of Big Brother.

Thought Police: The Party's army of secret agents charged with investigating and arresting suspected enemies of the State.

Two Minutes Hate: A daily ritual intended to stir up antipathy for the Party's war enemies—especially Emmanuel Goldstein, a counter-revolutionary figure.

Critical Response

- A Locus All-Time Best SF Novel winner
- A Prometheus Hall of Fame Award winner
- A BSFA Best Media nominee

"Orwell's novel escorts us so quietly, so directly, and so dramatically from our own day to the fate which may be ours in the future, that the experience is a blood-chilling one." —*Saturday Review*

"It is probable that no other work of this generation has made us desire freedom more earnestly or loathe tyranny with such fullness." —Mark Shorer, *The New York Times*

"*Nineteen Eighty-Four* is a remarkable book; as a virtuoso literary performance it has a sustained brilliance that has rarely been matched in other works of its genre. . . . It is as timely as the label on a poison bottle."   —*New York Herald Tribune*

About George Orwell

Considered one of the greatest writers of the twentieth century, George Orwell was an English journalist and novelist. Born Eric Arthur Blair in Motihari, Bengal, India, in 1903, his father was a civil servant who remained absent most of his childhood. After Orwell's birth, his mother returned to England with the children. Young George attended a boarding school in Eastbourne. It was there that he had his first taste of upper-class social status, never quite feeling he fit in amongst his privileged classmates. However, he went on to win a scholarship to the prestigious Eton College near Windsor, England. It's widely believed that these early experiences were a major influence on his future commitment to social and class justice.

Orwell joined the India Imperial Police Force in 1922. It was during this period that he launched a successful writing career, with stints as a BBC correspondent and a freedom fighter against Franco's fascist regime in Spain. In 1938, he was diagnosed with tuberculosis, a disease he would fight for the rest of his life. The publication of his famous satire, *Animal Farm*, came in 1945, followed by his masterwork, *1984*, in 1949. Shortly thereafter, he married his second wife, Sonia Brownell, but succumbed to tuberculosis a year later.

For Your Information

Online

"10 Books Like '1984.'" ThePortalist.com

"George Orwell's 1984 is a best-seller again. Here's why it resonates now." PBS.org

"George Orwell's '1984' is Suddenly a Best-Seller." NYTimes.com

"The masterpiece that killed George Orwell." TheGuardian.com

"The Message for Today in Orwell's '1984.'" NYTimes.com

"Required Reading: 10 Classic High School Books to Read Again." EarlyBirdBooks.com

Books

Big Brother: The Orwellian Nightmare Come True by Mark Dice

Catch-22 by Joseph Heller

Fahrenheit 451 by Ray Bradbury

Orwell: The Life by D. J. Taylor

Other Books by George Orwell

Animal Farm

Burmese Days

Down and Out in Paris (published under his real name, Eric Blair)

Homage to Catalonia

Keep the Aspidistra Flying

Politics and the English Language

Why I Write

Bibliography

"1984: George Orwell's road to dystopia." *BBC.com*, February 8, 2013. http://www.bbc.com/news /magazine-21337504.

de Freytas-Tamura, Kimiko. "George Orwell's '1984' is Suddenly a Best-Seller." *New York Times*, January 25, 2017. https://www.nytimes.com/2017/01/25 /books/1984-george-orwell-donald-trump.html.

"George Orwell Biography, Author, Journalist (1903– 1950)." *Biography*, August 11, 2016. http://www .biography.com/people/george-orwell-9429833.

McCrum, Robert. "The masterpiece that killed George Orwell." *The Guardian*, May 9, 2009. https://www.theguardian.com/books/2009 /may/10/1984-george-orwell.

WORTH BOOKS
SMART SUMMARIES

So much to read, so little time?

Explore summaries of bestselling fiction and essential nonfiction books on a variety of subjects, including business, history, science, lifestyle, and much more.

MORE SMART SUMMARIES
FROM WORTH BOOKS

CLASSIC FICTION

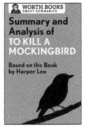

MORE SMART SUMMARIES
FROM WORTH BOOKS

TRENDING

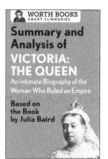

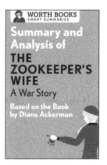

WORTH BOOKS
SMART SUMMARIES

OPEN  ROAD

INTEGRATED MEDIA

Lightning Source UK Ltd.
Milton Keynes UK
UKHW011836270421
382716UK00002B/482